This Little Tiger book belongs to:

_____

_____

_____

LITTLE TIGER PRESS LTD,
an imprint of the Little Tiger Group,
1 Coda Studios, 189 Munster Road, London SW6 6AW
www.littletiger.co.uk

First published in Great Britain 2016
This edition published 2017

Concept by Maudie Powell-Tuck and Dana Brown
Text by Maudie Powell-Tuck
Text copyright © Little Tiger Press Ltd 2016
Illustrations copyright © Richard Smythe 2016
Richard Smythe has asserted his right to be identified as the illustrator of
this work under the Copyright, Designs and Patents Act, 1988

A CIP catalogue record for this book is available from the British Library

All rights reserved · ISBN 978-1-84869-885-7

Printed in China · LTP/1800/3356/0620

4 6 8 10 9 7 5 3

For Dana, the other half of Team Messy Book
– M P T

For Henry, Darcey and Gertruda
– R S

The MESSY BOOK

Maudie Powell-Tuck • Richard Smythe

LITTLE TIGER
LONDON

I've made a mess.

Maybe you should tidy it up?

Maybe. Or we could just . . .

But tidying is *boring*.

We could hide the mess under my bed . . .

or blow it up . . .

. . . or eat it.

That is NOT proper tidying.

RUMBLE
RUMBLE
RUMBLE